Delphine Denise and the Mardi Gras Prize

Brittany Mazique
illustrated by Sawyer Cloud

Albert Whitman & Company
Chicago, Illinois

To my mom, the real Delphine Denise. And my dad, my reason for falling for New Orleans.—BM

To every child; your dreams are valid no matter where you come from.—SC

Library of Congress Cataloging-in-Publication data is on file with the publisher.
Text copyright © 2022 by Brittany Mazique
Illustrations copyright © 2022 by Albert Whitman & Company
Illustrations by Sawyer Cloud
First published in the United States of America in 2022
by Albert Whitman & Company
ISBN 978-0-8075-1548-8 (hardcover)
ISBN 978-0-8075-1547-1 (ebook)
Printed in China
10 9 8 7 6 5 4 3 2 1 RRD 26 25 24 23 22 21

Design by Rick DeMonico

For more information about Albert Whitman & Company, visit our website at www.albertwhitman.com.

I'm Delphine Denise Debreaux, and I have a few favorite things:
New Orleans, because that's where I live.
Purple, green, *and* gold, because it's impossible to choose just one color.

And Mardi Gras, because it's the **BIGGEST** celebration
of the year!

My friends and I always march together in the Mardi Gras parade. Getting ready is part of the fun.

We make masks with fancy feathers. And colorful costumes with beads and boas.

We decorate our bikes with streamers and balloons.

And we bake a delicious king cake topped with sprinkles, to eat after the parade.

But this year the Mardi Gras parade will be **BIGGER** than ever.
There's a **BIG, SHINY** grand prize for the best float!

BEST MARDI GRAS FLOAT
CONTEST
GRAND PRIZE
"A CROWN"

If that crown were mine, I'd wear it...

When riding through town on the streetcar.
While gobbling beignets in the French Quarter.
And while visiting Jackson Square, so all the
artists could paint my picture.

But there's one major problem.

Theodore frowns. "We don't know how to build a float."

Anna Louise shakes her head. "Every year we just ride our bikes."

"And we always have fun!" adds Xavier.

I *really* want to win that crown. "We can do it!" I say.

I get my wagon, which is just right for building a float. My friends help me paint. Cut. Color. We glue Mardi Gras decorations on my wagon until it is as dressed up as a carnival king.

Our float is **BIG** but not **BIG**
enough. "We need to think **BIGGER**,"
I say.

My friends watch without saying a word as I pile
things high on our wagon.
Ladders, for throwing beads to the crowds.

Pots, pans, and even a stove, to boil crawfish.
And cymbals, drums, and saxophones, because
Mardi Gras is all about good music.

When I'm done, Xavier points to the sagging float. Anna Louise squints at me. Theodore stomps his foot. "Delphine Denise, our float will *never* float," he says.

I cross my arms over my chest. "Do you want to win that crown? Or **NOT**?"

My friends all look at one another.

"Riding on a float that won't float isn't fun," says Xavier.

"We just want to have a good time," adds Anna Louise.

"Why don't we ride our bikes, like we always do?"

"Who cares about some silly prize?" asks Theodore.

"I do," I say firmly. "I'll just march by myself."

"If that's what you want," sighs Xavier. "The parade won't be the same without you."

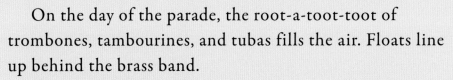

On the day of the parade, the root-a-toot-toot of
trombones, tambourines, and tubas fills the air. Floats line
up behind the brass band.

Crowds on both sides of the street are ready to catch
colorful beads and shiny coins.

The sun is beaming. It's the perfect day to win a **BIG**,
SHINY crown!

"Happy Mardi Gras!" I shout to the crowd.
I steer my **GRAND** float past my friends and wave.
That's when things take a turn for the worse...

First, a pot.

Then, a pan.

I steer with one hand and catch things with the other as they tumble off my float.

A wheel comes loose. Then another!

"Watch out, Delphine Denise!" shouts
Anna Louise.

"Do you need our help?" asks Xavier.

"Everything's fine!" I yell back.

Theodore shrugs. "If you say so."

Then...

BOOM!
CRASH!
KERPLUNK!
The parade rolls on past me.
My favorite celebration of the year is ruined!
I'll never win that big, shiny crown now.

And my friends are having fun without me.

But maybe...I can still convince them to have fun *with* me.

I sprint to the kitchen. I can still save our favorite part of Mardi Gras.

I grab a bowl and add eggs, milk, sugar, and flour. Then I start mixing. I put my concoction in the oven. When it's done baking, I add the finishing touch.

After I place the last sprinkle, I run fast to find my friends, and the words tumble out of me.

"I'm so sorry! I don't need a fancy float or a big old crown to have fun. Next year, it's back to our traditions, like..."

I show them my surprise. "King cake!"

Everyone takes a giant bite. No one can resist a good king cake.

"Now **THIS** is a good time!" I say, my mouth full of cake. "Who needs a silly crown, anyway?"

"Well..." whispers Theodore.
"About that," adds Anna Louise.
"Ta-da!" shouts Xavier.

My eyes get **BIG**! My very own crown. My friends
made it for me in **ALL** of my favorite colors.

"It's just like the grand prize from the parade,"
says Theodore.

"It's even better," I say.

Author's Note

Born and raised in Memphis, Tennessee, I spent many of my awkward middle-school days visiting my dad in New Orleans, Louisiana. It's the only city I know where taking a jaunt on the trolley, noshing on pralines, or strolling through the French Quarter on a hot and humid day feels like an adventure. When I decided to tell underrepresented stories of African Americans, I knew I wanted them to take place in settings rich with our unique historical and cultural experiences.

A voracious reader at an early age, I discovered most of my favorite characters did not share my skin color. Craving characters like Eloise, with their bold, fun, and sassy personalities, but wanting them to look like me, I reimagined them that way instead. Later, as a mother of my own precocious little brown girls, Margaux and Millie, I created Delphine Denise. My mom, who was lively, vivacious, and always up to good trouble as a child, was my inspiration. I celebrate her life and the stories of marginalized children with Delphine Denise. Sparking the imagination of all readers, with literary escapes that leave them inspired, proud, and thankful for who they are, is my hope.

Mardi Gras in New Orleans

Mardi Gras is a Christian holiday marking the last Tuesday before Lent. During Lent, Christians fast or give up bad habits for forty days. Mardi Gras means "Fat Tuesday" in French, and the holiday is a celebration—one last day of fun before Lent begins.

In New Orleans, the whole city is lively during Mardi Gras, or Carnival, season. The first Mardi Gras in New Orleans was celebrated in 1699 with fancy balls. In the late nineteenth century, people began throwing colorful beads and fake jewels from parade floats during Mardi Gras; carnival kings were said to be throwing gems to their loyal subjects in the crowd.

Mardi Gras's official colors are purple, for justice; gold, for power; and green, for faith. In a traditional Mardi Gras parade, streets are filled with elaborately decorated floats, and people march to the sound of brass bands while twirling parasols or handkerchiefs, yelling, "Laissez les bon temps rouler!" This is French for "Let the good times roll!"

Mardi Gras is more than fun-filled festivities and parades, though. It is a time when all people—young and old, rich and poor, from all different races—come together to celebrate.

New Orleans Words and Phrases

bayou: A body of water in a flat, low area, usually connected to a lake or river, and home to shrimp, catfish, alligators, crocodiles, crawfish, toads, and turtles.

beignet: Fried portions of dough, like doughnuts but without the hole. They are served piping hot and covered in powdered sugar—and they're always delicious!

Café du Monde: A coffee shop famous for its scrumptious beignets, mouthwatering hot chocolate, and strong coffee, located in New Orleans's French Market.

crawfish: This Louisiana staple goes by many names, such as crayfish, crawdaddy, or mudbug. But don't let their funny names fool you—these mini lobster-like crustaceans pack some serious flavor and can be found in many New Orleans dishes.

French Quarter: The "Crown Jewel" of New Orleans; a vibrant neighborhood of colorful buildings with cast-iron balconies, historic homes, one-of-a-kind shops, and restaurants serving all of the most popular dishes in New Orleans.

gumbo: A popular creole stew made of yummy spices, crawfish, sausage, shrimp, and okra. It's the official state dish of Louisiana.

Jackson Square: An old square in the heart of the French Quarter, where portrait artists, mimes, musicians, and jugglers gather to entertain crowds.

king cake: Imagine a cinnamon roll with purple, green, and gold icing and sprinkles on top. Twist that dough into an oval shape, and you've got yourself a king cake!

second line: The people carrying parasols, waving handkerchiefs, and dancing to the music following the brass band in a parade.

streetcar: From St. Charles Avenue to the French Quarter and beyond, old-fashioned trolley cars transport tourists and New Orleans natives alike. It's a fun and easy way to take in the sights and sounds of New Orleans!